A Lucas/Spielberg Presentation

THE LAND BEFORE TIME™

A Don Bluth Film

THE SEARCH FOR THE GREAT VALLEY

Adapted by Jim Razzi · From a Story by Judy Freudberg and Tony Geiss
Screenplay by Stu Krieger · Illustrations from the Don Bluth Film

PICTURE CORGI BOOKS

The bright white circle shone high in the sky as a family of long-necks wandered across a barren plain in search of food. The youngest, who was called Littlefoot, munched on some pine needles and made a face.

"I hate pine needles!" Littlefoot cried.

His mother looked at him patiently and said, "When we reach the Great Valley, there will be plenty of good food for us to eat."

"But where is it?" cried Littlefoot. "We've been travelling so long. How do you know it's really there?"

His mother answered, "Some things you see with your eyes. Others you see with your heart."

Just then, Littlefoot's mother spied a beautiful star-shaped leaf hanging by itself from a high branch of a nearby tree. Reaching up, she plucked it off and gave it to Littlefoot. Littlefoot's eyes went wide with delight. But he decided not to eat it. As delicious as the leaf might taste, it was so beautiful that he wanted to save it.

Littlefoot left the tree star behind when he found a little three-horn named Cera to play with in a nearby swamp. And the leaf went even further from his thoughts when a huge monster suddenly appeared at the edge of the swamp. It was Sharptooth, the most feared and ferocious creature in the land. Littlefoot and Cera tried to hide, but it was no use. Sharptooth saw them and attacked, ripping everything in sight.

Littlefoot's mother came to their rescue. With one mighty swipe of her big tail, she knocked the monster aside. Sharptooth roared in anger and turned to attack her. Littlefoot and Cera watched in horror as Sharptooth and Littlefoot's mother fought a desperate battle.

When it seemed certain that Sharptooth was winning, Littlefoot's mother gave him another powerful whack and knocked him to the ground. "Run now, Littlefoot!" she cried. "I will follow."

Littlefoot and Cera ran into a small canyon, looking for a place to hide. Suddenly the ground under their feet began to tremble and crack. It was an earthquake!

All the creatures on the plain fled for their lives, including Sharptooth. He raced towards Littlefoot and Cera just as a gigantic crack widened behind them. The ground tilted, and the three of them tumbled towards a deep hole, with Littlefoot and Cera falling onto Sharptooth's head.

Sharptooth tried to bite them, but Littlefoot's mother once more arrived just in time and knocked Sharptooth into the jagged hole. Littlefoot and Cera went sailing up into the air.

Just as they were about to fall, Littlefoot's mother caught them and carried them to safety. But then the ground trembled and shook again, and in the confusion that followed, Cera vanished and so did Littlefoot's mother.

Littlefoot had to wait until the earthquake was over before he could look for his mother. As he wandered the stricken land he cried out, "Mother, where are you?" His voice came echoing back to him.

At last he found her, lying silently on the broken ground. She had been hurt very badly by Sharptooth.

"Littlefoot," she said painfully, "you must find the Great Valley by yourself. Just follow the bright circle to where it touches the earth. Look for the great rock in the shape of a long-neck and for the mountains that burn."

Then she laid her head down and became very still. Littlefoot nuzzled his mother and felt the tears come to his eyes. He was really all alone now.

"I don't care if I never get to the Great Valley," he said. "I just want you back."

As Littlefoot sadly moved away, the tree star, which he had totally forgotten, appeared in the sky and fluttered down next to him. Glancing up, he looked with disbelief at a cloud shaped like his mother. And then her voice seemed to come to him on the wind.

"I'll be with you even if you can't see me. I'll be in your heart," it said. "Follow your heart."

Even though he still hurt inside, he took courage from hearing his mother's voice. He wiped away his tears, held the tree star close, and bravely set out to find the Great Valley.

A short time later he came to the rim of a canyon and saw someone he knew. It was Cera.

"Will you come with me to look for the Great Valley?" asked Littlefoot.

"I'm going my own way," said Cera. "I don't believe the Great Valley even exists."

"My mother told me about it," said Littlefoot. "And I believe her. If you don't believe in anything, what's the use of going on?"

But Cera only scrambled down into the canyon. For a moment Littlefoot wondered if he had been talking to himself as much as to Cera. But then he remembered what his mother had said about following his heart. So he sniffed back a tear and continued on his lonely journey.

Littlefoot soon made two new friends—a little big-mouth named Ducky and
a baby flier named Petrie—who believed his story about the Great Valley. They
even begged to come along with him. Littlefoot felt much better. With high hopes,
he and his two new friends marched off across the barren land.

Although Petrie was a flier, he insisted he couldn't fly. Instead he perched
himself on top of Littlefoot's head and tucked the tree star under his wing for
safekeeping.

That night the three travellers heard a screaming creature coming closer and closer—until it ran right into them. It was Cera. Breathlessly she told them she had met Sharptooth down in the canyon where she had been.

"He's still alive!" she cried. "And he will come after us! Just you wait and see!"

Littlefoot said that Cera just wanted everyone to worry more about Sharptooth than about reaching the Great Valley.

Soon a little spike-tail, whom Ducky named Spike, joined the weary group. That night they lay down, exhausted, in a nice snug hole. In no time they were sleeping soundly.

But in the morning they woke to find that the snug hole was really Sharptooth's footprint! Through the morning fog they could see the gigantic creature searching for them.

"It's Sharptooth," whispered Cera. "I told you he would come."

The group made such a racket getting up that the monster heard them. With a terrible roar that shook the air, he charged into their midst.

They all screamed and ran, but Sharptooth cut them off at every turn.

"I will lead him away!" cried Littlefoot.

Littlefoot dashed off in a different direction with Petrie clinging to his head and holding the tree star. Sharptooth roared after them. In fright, Petrie dropped the tree star. The beast crushed it under his huge feet as he closed in for the kill.

At the last moment Littlefoot ran through a crevice in some rocks that was too small for Sharptooth.

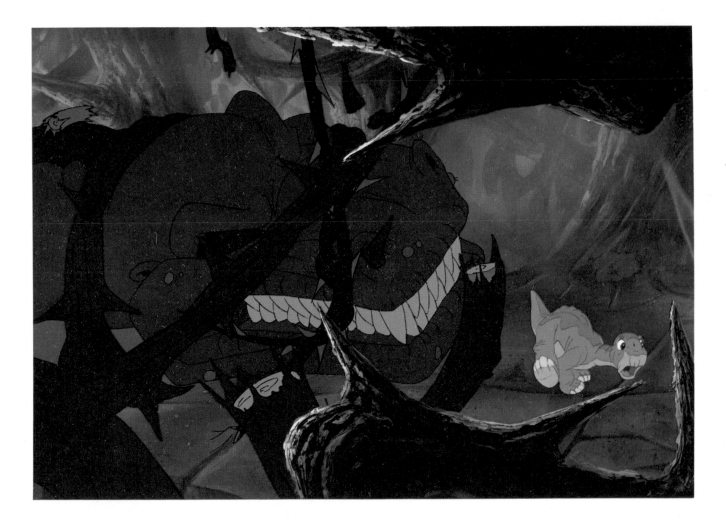

Littlefoot joined the others in safety. "We made it!" he shouted.

"Yes, but tree star gone," said Petrie sadly.

Littlefoot choked back a sob. His mother's gift was gone forever, and without it he felt lonelier than ever.

As he stood gazing into the distance he saw a large rock shaped like a long-neck. "Look!" he shouted. "We're going the right way. Don't give up hope now!"

The group obediently trudged on, but in spite of what Littlefoot had said, they were losing hope.

After dragging themselves over a rocky plain and through an ash storm caused by the burning mountains, the weary little band of travellers found themselves at the bottom of a huge crater. They were so tired that they wanted to give up.

"How can you give up now?" cried Littlefoot. "What would you do anyway? Where would you go? Maybe the Great Valley is just over this ridge."

"I still don't believe it even exists," said Cera angrily.

"I do," answered Littlefoot. "I have faith. I follow my heart."

Cera laughed. "You're just a dumb long-neck, then," she said. "How can you have faith in something you've never seen?"

"My mother had faith," answered Littlefoot, getting angry.

"Well, she was a dumb long-neck, too!" cried Cera.

Littlefoot charged at Cera, and the two of them had a terrible fight.

When Littlefoot and Cera finally stopped their battle, Cera announced, "I'm going my own way. Anyone who wants to come with me is welcome."

One by one they left Littlefoot and joined Cera—even Petrie. He looked at Littlefoot sadly and said, "Maybe Cera right. I can no see Great Valley either."

"Yep, that's true," agreed Ducky. "Great Valley must be great dream, yep, yep, yep."

"Fine!" cried Littlefoot, hurt and angry. "Go off by yourselves, all of you. I don't need any of you."

So once more Littlefoot found himself alone and downhearted. But he forced himself to go on.

"Mother didn't tell me it would be this hard to follow my heart," he said to himself out loud.

Over hill and mountain and plain he trudged. But the Great Valley never appeared. He wasn't even sure *he* believed in it anymore. He wiped away a tear.

After climbing up a jagged hill, he found himself overlooking a great plain. He looked up at the sky. A pink-and-grey cloud was slowly drifting by. It looked like his mother. His mind told him that it was only a cloud, no more and no less. But his heart cried out to it anyway.

"I've tried to do what you told me, Mother," he wailed. "But it's too hard to believe in what you can't see."

The cloud drifted by, and suddenly he seemed to hear his mother's voice on the wind. "My dear Littlefoot," it said. "Sometimes hope is dimmest just when you are near the light. Don't give up."

Then the cloud began to drift further away.

"Don't go, Mother!" Littlefoot cried.

All at once, beneath the cloud, he saw an opening through a far mountain wall. And beyond that he could see a beautiful land. It was the Great Valley!

He dashed towards it, not thinking of anything but his own joy at finding the valley. But the wind swirled and he heard his mother's voice whispering again.

"Littlefoot . . . "

"The others . . . they went the wrong way," Littlefoot said. "They'll never find the Great Valley by themselves. Mother, what should I do?" But he already knew the answer.

"My heart . . . " he murmured. "My heart tells me they're my friends. I have to help them. Without me to show them the way, they have no hope. And I have learned that this is the most terrible thing of all."

The cloud image of his mother started to break up even as he watched. "You don't need me anymore," it said.

Littlefoot smiled and nodded. "I will find them, Mother!" he cried. "And I will lead them here to the Great Valley!" Then he looked up at the blue sky and added, "You will be in my heart forever, Mother."

"And you will be in mine, dear Littlefoot," the wind whispered as he turned and headed back to his friends.